A cap seller went to market.

The gibbons took caps from his bag.

The cap seller shouted and stamped his feet.

The gibbons shouted and stamped, too.

The clever cap seller had a plan.

He dropped his cap on the ground.

The gibbons dropped the caps, too.

The cap seller picked up the caps and went to market.